THE REMARKABLE
JOURNEY
OF
GUSTAVUS BELL

THE REMARKABLE JOURNEY OF GUSTAVUS BELL

GLORIA SKURZYNSKI

Illustrated by
Tim and Greg Hildebrandt

Nashville • ABINGDON PRESS • *New York*

Library of Congress Cataloging in Publication Data
Skurzynski, Gloria.
The remarkable journey of Gustavus Bell.

SUMMARY: When he is suddenly stricken by the
rare halving disease, Gustavus meets progressively
smaller animals, from dogs to aphids, in his search
for help.
[1. Humorous stories. 2. Fantasy] I. Hildebrandt,
Tim, illus. II. Hildebrandt, Greg, illus. III. Title.
PZ7. S6287Re   [Fic]   72-6168
ISBN 0-687-36122-2

For Ed and our daughters

THE REMARKABLE
JOURNEY
OF
GUSTAVUS BELL

It was an ordinary August day. It was a day so ordinary, in fact, that when Gustavus Bell saw the book *Extraordinary Diseases the World Over* on the library shelf, he decided to check it out.

"On a day as ordinary as this," he explained to the librarian, "I need something extra-ordinary to liven things up, even if it's only a book about weird diseases."

He tossed the book into his bicycle basket and began to pedal slowly along the hot asphalt street toward his home, seven blocks away. On every lawn along every street whirleybird sprinklers flung out water in wide circles, or rainbird sprinklers spit out water in irregular arcs. The citizens of Canyon Rim were waging their annual battle to keep their lawns green, battling against the hot, high, relentless Western sun.

Gustavus scratched his head. His hair felt hot beneath his fingers.

"Always wear a hat when you're out in the afternoon sun," his mother had told him over and over again. "Even if it's just your baseball cap, always keep your head covered. If you don't, this desert sun will fry your brains." Gustavus had forgotten to wear a hat, as usual, on this particular August day.

The street in front of him seemed to separate into two halves which looked exactly the same. Gustavus stared in amazement. "I wonder if my brains are already beginning to fry," he thought. He shut his eyes and shook his head to clear his vision. When he opened his eyes, the street looked normal again.

"Wow! I'd better get home and get out of the sun," he said to himself. He began to pedal faster, but his knees felt weak and rubbery. He coasted into his driveway and dropped his bike on the lawn, even though his father had forbidden him to leave his bike there. "I'll put it away later," he told his dog Fearless, who had come out to greet him, wagging his tail and whining in welcome. The dog jumped against Gustavus and Gustavus staggered, almost falling against the red brick wall of his house.

"Fearless, cut it out!" he scolded. "You're going to knock me over. There's something wrong with me. I think I got too much sun."

As he walked across the lawn, Gustavus felt as though his feet were sinking into soft cotton fluff. The ground seemed to rise and fall beneath him like ocean waves. The library book which he held in his arms grew unbearably heavy. He pushed open the back door, fell into a chair, and dropped his aching head onto the cool formica surface of the kitchen table.

"Anyone home?" He meant it to be a shout, but it came out a whisper. His forehead was resting on the edge of a piece of paper. When he raised his head a few inches, the letters on the piece of paper danced before his eyes.

"Dear Gustavus—I'll be gone all afternoon decorating the church basement for the bazaar tonight. Your lunch is in the refrigerator. At four o'clock please turn on the oven to 350 degrees. Love, Mother."

"Just like a mother," he thought. "They're never around when you need them."

He stood up unsteadily, clutching his book with his left hand, holding with his right hand to the edge of the table, then onto the backs of the kitchen chairs, afraid to let go because he might fall. He slid his hand along the wall for support as he crept toward his bedroom. By the time he dropped onto his bed, his head was spinning alarmingly. Fearless jumped beside him on the bed, whining and licking Gustavus' cheek.

"Boy, Fearless," he moaned, "I feel awful. Stay here with me . . . will you, old pal . . . so that if I die I won't die alone." He kicked off his sneakers. In less than a minute he was asleep.

When he woke up he still felt dizzy, only not as much. He stretched out on the cool cotton bedspread, expecting to feel the maple headboard at his fingertips and the maple footboard pressing against his toes. All he felt was the cool cotton bedspread. He stretched again, as far as he could stretch, but still his fingers and toes touched nothing but the bedspread. He sat up and looked around him. His bed looked enormous, twice as big as usual. Then he caught sight of Fearless snoozing at the foot of the bed. Gustavus nearly jumped off the mattress. Fearless was a big as he was!

"Gosh!" Gustavus whispered in awe. He hit the side of his head with the palm of his hand a few times to clear his vision, but everything around him continued to look huge.

"Gosh!" he said aloud. "The whole room has doubled in size!"

Fearless opened his eyes, raised his head, and yawned, curling his pink tongue. "The room hasn't doubled in size, Gustavus," the dog said. "It's you. You've shrunk in half."

"Fearless!" Gustavus shrieked. "You're talking! When did you learn to talk?"

"I guess I've always known how to talk," the dog answered, lowering his head modestly, "but I never before had anything important to say. But this is important. I saw you shrink. You were tossing and moaning in your sleep, and then—poof! You were only half as big as before."

"I must have some really weird disease," Gustavus said, shaking his head.

"An extraordinary disease, would you say?" Fearless asked.

"A super extraordinary disease."

"Then why don't you look it up in that book you brought home?" the dog suggested.

"That's a great idea," Gustavus said, looking for the book. "You're really a smart dog. But one thing surprises me, Fearless. I mean, I'm really surprised that you can talk at all, but since you're a Siberian Husky, I'd expect

12

you to talk in Siberian. But instead you're talking in English."

"Don't be silly, Gustavus," the dog replied. "My ancestors have lived in the United States for generations. Why should I speak Siberian? After all, your great-grandparents came here from Sweden, and you don't speak Swedish, do you? No one would ever guess that your sire had a Swedish pedigree, except for that ridiculous name they gave you—Gustavus!"

"I was named after my grandfather," Gustavus murmured apologetically. "But you're right, Fearless. I'm just not thinking logically. It's this dizziness in my head. Now where did that library book go?"

"Look on the floor," the dog said, yawning again.

"Oh yes. There it is." The floor looked very far away. "How am I going to get down there?"

"Turn around and slide down on your belly, feet first, like a baby does," Fearless suggested.

"This is ridiculous," Gustavus said, sliding to the floor. "I'm not much bigger than a baby. Do I look like a baby, Fearless?"

"No. You look like your normal self, only half as big."

Gustavus tried to lift the book, but it was heavy, so he sprawled on the floor and opened the cover to the index. "What should I look under?" He ran his finger down through the long list of extraordinary diseases. "Here's something! 'Halving disease.' Does that sound like what I've got?"

"It's a good possibility," the dog replied. "Look it up."

"Page 218." Gustavus turned the big pages with difficulty. "Here it is. 'Halving disease, medical name *Hemi-*

somatiasis. First observed and recorded in Prague, Czechoslovakia, by Dr. Anton Zidek in 1923. Symptoms —fever, dizziness, weakness of the knees, fatigue, and a sudden diminishing of height and girth by half, hence the common name, halving disease.' " He looked up. "That sounds like what I have, all right."

"Keep reading," Fearless said.

" 'The cause of halving disease has not yet been de-termined, although an unidentified virus is suspected. The victim suffers continuing spells of fever and dizziness. After each spell, the body shrinks to half the previous size. The reduction in size is very precise—thus, a man six feet tall will shrink first to three feet, then to one and a half feet, and so on.' "

Gustavus looked up and narrowed his eyes. "Let's see. I'm five feet tall, or at least I was, so if I shrank in half I must be two and a half feet tall right now."

"Does it say anything else in the book?" Fearless asked.

"Let me look." Gustavus studied the page again and turned pale. "It says, 'There is no known treatment for halving disease.' Good grief, Fearless! Does that mean I'm going to spend the rest of my life two and a half feet tall?"

"No-o-o-o," Fearless answered slowly, "that's not the impression I get. It sounds to me as though you're going to keep on shrinking smaller and smaller."

"Oh-oh! I think maybe you're right. I'm beginning to get awfully dizzy again. . . ."

"Hang on there, Gustavus."

Gustavus curled his fingers over the edge of the book as the room spun like a leaf in a whirlpool. When his head cleared, he was lying flat on his stomach on page 218. He was astonished to notice that the book was only

14

three inches shorter in length than he was. He calculated rapidly. "If I was two and a half feet tall the last time, I must be one and a quarter feet tall now. That's fifteen inches. Fearless, what am I going to do?"

"I'd say you'd better get some help."

"But how? I can't reach the telephone, and even if I could, I couldn't lift the receiver or dial. My mother! I've got to get to my mother!"

"Where is she?"

"She's in the basement of the church, decorating for a bazaar."

"At the church, huh?" Fearless grunted. "I'd say that's a pretty long walk for a little fellow fifteen inches high."

"Will you take me there, Fearless? I could climb on your back and ride all the way. I won't be very heavy. I can't weigh very much now."

"Of course I'll take you there, Gustavus. Glad to do it. We Siberian Huskies were bred as working dogs, you know. My ancestors used to pull whole Eskimo families on sleds. I'll lay down on the floor and you climb up on my back."

"That's *lie* down, Fearless. You should say, I'll *lie* down on the floor."

"You're really something, Gustavus, you know that?" the dog asked. "You've got a dog who talks and who's going to carry you on a rescue mission, and you worry about grammar."

Gustavus blushed. "I'm sorry, Fearless. You're right. I shouldn't have said that."

"Well, never mind. Hurry up and climb on my back before you shrink some more."

Without too much difficulty, Gustavus climbed on

Fearless' back and held onto his collar. "Okay, boy, let's go."

"I'll have to go through my doggie door," Fearless explained, "so you'd better lie as flat as you can against my back. Otherwise you might get bruised when the door scrapes against you."

Fearless crouched as low as he could when he wiggled through the opening in the back door, but nevertheless Gustavus' back was stung where the swinging panel brushed against him.

Gustavus held tightly as Fearless trotted across the back porch onto the lawn. When they emerged from the shade of the porch, the full force of the hot sun made his head begin to spin once again.

"Stop, Fearless!" he shouted. "I think I'm having another shrinking spell." The dog stood still, and Gustavus held onto the collar with clenched fists, but his fingers were forced apart as the leather of the collar seemed to double in his hands.

"Gustavus, I'm worried," Fearless said. "If you keep shrinking while I'm running to the church, you might get so small that you'll fall off and get lost. Then what will we do?"

"You're right, Fearless. We'll have to think of something else. Put me down."

The dog lay down carefully on the warm grass. "Is this far enough, or do you want me to roll over?"

"Gosh no, Fearless, don't roll over! You'll crush me! I can slide down from your back the way I slid off the bed. Hold still for a minute."

Gustavus slid down the dog's side and landed on his knees in the warm grass. "Everything is so hot out here. I think the heat brought on that last shrinking spell."

"Then you'd better get into the shade. Hold onto my tail for support, and I'll walk you over to the cottonwood tree. There's plenty of shade beneath it."

They crossed the yard, and Gustavus sat with his back against the tree trunk. "I never realized what a long walk it is across the yard when you're small. I wonder how much smaller I'm going to get."

"Maybe if you sit still and don't exert yourself you won't shrink too much more," Fearless said. "I'll run to the church and get your mother. You stay right here beneath the tree so that we can find you when we get back, all right?"

"All right."

"Are you sure you'll be safe? I hate to leave you alone like this."

"Fearless, if you don't hurry and get my mother, I might not last too much longer. You're my only hope. Please stop standing around talking, and get going!"

"I'm off!" Fearless turned and raced across the lawn, through the driveway, and down the street. Then Gustavus lost sight of him.

The minutes seemed to drag endlessly. Gustavus began to get thirsty. The air was stifling, and the ground was hot even underneath the tree. He tried to think about something else, to get his mind off his increasing thirst, but he felt parched and miserable. He looked around and saw the garden faucet with the black rubber hose attached

18

to it. Big drops of water oozed slowly, very slowly, over the top edge of the hose connection and ran down the side of the hose to the grass below.

"If I could crawl carefully to that hose," Gustavus thought, "I could drink some of those drops to quench my thirst. If I don't move too suddenly, maybe I can get there and back without having another shrinking spell."

He dropped to his hands and knees and began to crawl through the grass. In a crawling position his back was even with the top edge of the blades of grass, which gave him some protection from the sun's fierce heat. He raised his head every now and then to take his bearings and to check on the direction of the water faucet.

The blades of grass were as thick as jungle. Gustavus' father prided himself on growing a thick, green, carpetlike lawn—no easy job in a town as dry as Canyon Rim. But at the moment Gustavus wished that the lawn were thinner and scragglier. He was using the top of his head to break a trail through the blades of grass when he heard a startled, "Oh my gracious to Betsy!"

He raised his head and found himself nose to nose with a soft, brown, furry, roly-poly creature with black, shiny, beady eyes.

"I beg your pardon," Gustavus said. "I didn't mean to startle you, Mr. Mouse. Or is it Mrs. Mouse?"

"Mouse!" The creature stood on its hind legs in indignation. "I am *not* a mouse!" It pirouetted around on tiptoe, revealing an underside covered with short gray fur, and a tail only an inch long. "Now do you recognize me?"

"I'm sorry," Gustavus said, "you still look like a mouse, only with a cutoff tail. Did you lose part of your tail in an accident?"

"Indeed!" The creature, exasperated, dropped to all

19

fours and glared at Gustavus. "I'm *supposed* to have a short tail. I am a field vole. My scientific name is *Arvicola agrestis,* but you may call me Mrs. Vole. It should have been obvious to you that I am not an ordinary mouse, you stupid little boy."

"I am not a stupid little boy," Gustavus retorted, drawing himself up to his full seven and a half inches. "I have an I.Q. of a hundred and forty."

Mrs. Vole sniffed. "I have no idea what my own I.Q. is, but I suspect it's rather high. No one ever bothers to measure the I.Q. of voles. Instead they're always testing those silly white laboratory mice. As if it's any indication of intelligence to race through a maze the way those white mice do—just to get a drop of sugar water. A vole would never bother. Besides, sugar water rots the teeth."

"Speaking of water," Gustavus said, "I'm terribly thirsty. That's why I started over here in the first place, to get a drink of the water dripping from that hose."

He walked the remaining distance to the faucet and hose and stood watching the drops run down the underside of the hose, one after the other. "I suppose I'll just have to stand here and catch the drops in my mouth as they roll by."

He opened his mouth, stuck out his tongue, and waited for the next drop. It hit his mouth with a splash.

"Aaaagh!" he yelled.

The water tasted terrible. It had the taste of hot black rubber hose. Gustavus spit it out, his face screwed up in disgust.

"I could have told you that would taste awful," Mrs. Vole said, "but I didn't bother. Young folks never listen to grown-ups nowadays, anyway. Come along with me, if you like, into my nest. There's an underground leak in

20

the faucet pipe, and it drains into my home. I have my own private reservoir, and the water is cool and fresh. You can quench your thirst there."

"That's very kind of you, Mrs. Vole," Gustavus said.

"Yes, I know it is. But before we go, do you mind if I ask you one question? Why are you so short? I've seen lots of human children, but I've never seen one as short as you."

"I have a strange condition called halving disease," Gustavus explained. "Ever so often I shrink into half my former size."

"Oh. Is it contagious?" she asked anxiously. "I have four little children at home, and I'd hate to expose them to something they might catch."

"I don't think it's contagious, Mrs. Vole. And I think it's just a disease for human beings, anyway."

"All right, then. But just to be on the safe side, you'd better not stay too long. Follow me."

She ran along the grass for a short distance and then disappeared. When Gustavus crawled to where he had last seen her, he discovered a hole leading underground.

"Follow me!" Mrs. Vole's muffled voice drifted back through the opening. "There's a tricky crisscross network of underground tunnels in here, so you'd better stay right behind me or you'll get lost."

Gustavus dropped to his belly and snaked through the opening in the ground. The tunnel was so dark that he couldn't see a thing.

"Mrs. Vole," he called, "say something again so I can follow the sound of your voice."

"Hal-loooooo!" she shouted, just ahead of him. "I'll just keep talking so you can hear my voice. My husband says I'm the greatest nonstop talker in the entire animal

21

kingdom anyway." She laughed. "But of course he's just teasing. Actually we get along very well together, Mr. Vole and I. But you won't be able to meet Mr. Vole today. He's out gathering provisions. I must say, he's always been an excellent provider for as long as we've been married. Too bad you won't be able to meet him today. You'd like him. As I said, we've always got along very well together. My only complaint, and it's a very minor one, is that sometimes he's a little too strict with the kiddies. But then, all fathers are like that to a certain extent, I suppose."

With her last words Mrs. Vole reached the underground room which was her home. She turned and grasped Gustavus' hand with her humanlike paws and pulled him into the room. "It's a little brighter in here than in the tunnel. We have a small skylight, and enough daylight filters through it that we can see fairly well. Your eyes will adjust in just a minute." She turned and shouted, "Yoo-hoo, anybody home? Come out, children. We have a guest."

From each corner of the room a pair of black, beady eyes peered curiously at Gustavus. The vole children crept shyly to the center of the room and lined up beside their mother.

"These are my children," she announced proudly. "Three girls and a boy—Pansy, Daisy, Rosie, and Leif. Three flowers and a Leif."

"They're very nice children, Mrs. Vole," Gustavus said politely.

"Only four of them this time. It's the smallest litter I've ever had, but there's been so much talk about overpopulation. . . ." Her voice trailed off as she sighed and turned to her children. "Say hello to the short human boy, children. Where are your manners?"

"Hello," the four little voices squeaked.

"Oh, and where are *my* manners? I almost forgot why I invited you here. There's the drinking reservoir in the corner. Help yourself. You'll find it nice and cold. Actually, it makes the place rather damp and hard to heat in the winter, but in the summer it's just lovely."

Gustavus crossed to the pool of water in the corner of the room. He was so hot and thirsty that he plunged his mouth into the pool and drank long and deeply. When he stood up, he could feel the icy cold water coursing down into his stomach. Then his head began to spin. He clutched the root-entwined walls of the vole home for support.

"Oh-oh, it's happening again. Here I go!" he said, as he shrank in half.

"Mamma! What happened to him?" Rosie squealed.

"H-h-h-h-holy smokes!" Leif stammered.

"Mamma, I'm scared," Pansy wailed.

Daisy just stared, wide-eyed.

"Little boy, are you positive that this thing isn't contagious?" Mrs. Vole asked nervously.

"No, Ma'am, I can't be positive, but I'm the only one I know who's ever had it, so I didn't catch it from anyone. But if it will make you more comfortable, I'll leave right now."

"I hate to be an ungracious hostess," she said, "but a mother must always consider her children's welfare first of all, you understand."

"It's perfectly all right, Mrs. Vole. Don't apologize. I really do understand. My own mother would act the same way."

"I think I'd better stay here with the little girls, since they're so frightened," she said. "Leif, you take the boy

up through the tunnel passageway and put him out into the yard."

"Me?" Leif squeaked in alarm.

"Remember, Daddy said that you're to be the man of the house when he's not at home."

"All right," Leif said sullenly. "Come on, then. Stick right behind me, so you don't get lost in the tunnels."

"I'm sorry to be such a bother, Leif," Gustavus said, "but these spells always leave me weak and dizzy. I don't think I can make it through the tunnels if I have to crawl. Would you let me ride on your back?"

Leif scowled, but his mother gave him a look which meant, "Do anything you must to get him out of here."

"Oh all right," he grumbled. "Get on my back. You'll have to put your arms around my neck and lie as flat as you can, because these tunnels are pretty narrow."

Gustavus crawled on Leif's back and tried to put his arms around the little vole's neck, but it was hard to find his neck because it was as wide as the rest of his body.

Leif raced as fast as he could through the narrow passageway, bumping Gustavus roughly against the sides and the ceiling of the tunnel, making his ears ring alarmingly.

"Cut it out, Leif," he yelled. "If you don't quit banging me around, I'll fall off."

But Leif ran even faster. Gustavus' hands began to slip from Leif's neck. He tried to grab handfuls of hair, but the hair on Leif's back was so short and smooth that he couldn't hang on. At last, as he was sliding off Leif completely, he grabbed the little animal's short, stubby tail.

"Let go of my tail," Leif screamed. "Please let go!"

"Why? Does it hurt?"

"No, it doesn't hurt," Leif cried, still running. "Let go! Oh, please, let go. If you keep pulling my tail, you might stretch it, and then everyone would take me for an ordinary field mouse. My parents would die of shame!"

Gustavus ached all over from the rough ride Leif had given him, so he let go. The minute he fell to the floor of the tunnel, Leif turned tail and ran away, leaving Gustavus alone in the pitch-black darkness.

"I must be close to the mouth of the tunnel," he said to himself. "I'll just keep crawling along until I find my way out of here. But it's so dark, I can't see anything."

On his hands and knees he felt his way along the tunnel. It seemed easy enough at first, but then he came to an intersection where the tunnel branched off in three different directions. He had no idea which way to turn, so he decided to go straight ahead. As he crawled, he could feel the tunnel becoming narrower and narrower until he could barely squeeze through.

"I must have come in the wrong direction," he thought. He turned around to go back the way he came, but instead of reaching a wider tunnel, he came to an intersection where the tunnels branched off in six different directions. He chose the one which seemed widest and crawled through that one, but it, too, grew narrower the farther he crawled.

"Now I'm really lost," he said out loud.

Nearby he heard a rustling and a low whispering. "Is anyone here?" he asked.

26

"Alms for the poor," a soft voice said, and then another, and another voice joined in, saying, "Alms for the poor."

"Where are you?" Gustavus asked. "I can't see you."

"Are you blind, too?" a voice asked.

"No, I'm not blind. It's just so dark in here that I can't see anything."

"Who are you?" the voices asked.

"I'm Gustavus Bell. I'm a human being who happens to be very small at the moment. Who are you?"

The rustlings and whisperings grew closer. "We are the earth's poorest creatures. We are the dirt eaters. If you are a human, you must be rich. Give us something. Give us anything. Give us alms. Alms for the poor."

"I don't have anything to give," Gustavus replied. "I'm lost in these tunnels and I can't find my way out."

Gustavus could sense that the creatures were coming closer to him. "Give us some of your wealth, rich human," their voices said. "We are poor and blind. All other creatures despise us. We have nothing but dirt to eat. Alms for the poor, the poor, the poor. . . ."

A cold, slimy body touched Gustavus' hand and he screamed in terror. *"Get away from me! Who are you?"*

Slippery, clammy bodies surrounded him, writhing all around him. "We are the earthworms. We are the poor and downtrodden. Give us what you have."

Gustavus' heart pounded with fright. "I have nothing to give you," he shrieked. "Please leave me alone. I'm afraid of you!"

"Don't be afraid," the soft voices spoke in his ear. "We are only poor earthworms, the dirt eaters, the blind. Give us what you have and we won't hurt you."

"I have nothing to give," he sobbed. He curled himself in a ball to protect his skin from the slimy touch of the earthworms. He whimpered and quaked with fright. He had no idea how many earthworms surrounded him, whether it was five, or ten, or even a hundred. When something cold and wet touched his bare leg, he screamed and buried his head in his arms. Then warm fur covered him and a familiar voice called out, "It's all right, little boy. It's only me, Mrs. Vole. I bumped into you with my nose."

Gustavus turned and threw himself against the soft, warm body of Mrs. Vole. "Oh please," he sobbed, "get me out of here and away from these horrible worms."

Mrs. Vole grasped him around his waist with her paws and pulled him backwards along the narrow tunnel.

"I was afraid something like this would happen," she said. "When Leif told me he had left you alone in the tunnels, I knew you'd become lost, so I started out immediately to find you. I had such a hard time locating you! You certainly got off on the wrong track. And you're smaller again. You're only half as big as when you left my house."

"I guess I had another shrinking spell when the worms were crawling around me. I was so frightened!" Gustavus gasped. "My fear must have caused me to shrink again."

"My stars, you're still shaking! You're cold with fright. Cuddle up against me until you feel better." Mrs. Vole held him like a baby against her warm breast. In a few minutes his body stopped trembling.

"Do you feel better now?" she asked.

"Yes, Mrs. Vole. How can I ever thank you?"

"Tut, tut. Never mind. Now I'll take you out through the tunnels and see that you get safely into the sunlight.

Only this time, you go first. I'll stay behind you to make sure that you don't get lost again."

Mrs. Vole pushed Gustavus ahead of her through the intricate tunnel passageway until he could see a thin streak of daylight ahead.

"Here we are!" she announced brightly. "The end of the tunnel is just over there. Now you'll be safe."

Gustavus reached the mouth of the tunnel and gulped the sweet pure outside air deep into his lungs. Then he turned and took Mrs. Vole's paw. "I'll never forget you, Mrs. Vole. You've been very helpful and kind to me."

"I hope you reach home safely, little boy," she said. "Your mother must be very worried about you. Now I must return to my nest. I left the children alone, and my husband will soon be home for dinner. Also, I want to give Leif a spanking for deserting you in the tunnels. I was in such a hurry to find you that I didn't take time to give him the punishment he deserves. Good-bye, little boy. Take care, now."

"I will, Mrs. Vole. And thank you again." Gustavus watched Mrs. Vole retreat into the darkness of the tunnel. Then he turned and stepped through the narrow opening into the sunlight. He stood up and stretched his arms high above his head. It felt wonderful to be in the daylight again, although it was hard for his eyes to adjust to the brightness. He looked for the cottonwood tree and began to run toward it. After ten strides he stopped short, turned around, and dashed back in the direction from which he'd come, hurling himself head first into the mouth of the tunnel. He lay panting in the soft dirt until the furious beating of his heart slowed a bit. Then he poked his head cautiously above ground.

Hardly more than twenty paces away from him, a tarantula and a scorpion stood eye to eye in the hot sun, arguing furiously. They were so caught up in their violent discussion that neither of them had noticed Gustavus when he almost ran into them.

"Of course I'm dangerous," the tarantula was saying. "Just look at me. Don't I *look* dangerous? I'm the biggest spider in these parts, and I'm the hairiest spider in the whole United States of America. I'm so hairy I almost frighten people to death."

"Ha!" the scorpion scoffed. "That's all you can do—frighten people. You aren't poisonous enough to *bite* people to death. Now *I*—*I* can really sting! Look at my beautiful curved tail. The end of that tail is just loaded with poison!"

The tarantula danced on his long, hairy legs. "But look at me, look at all of me," he insisted. "Look at my hairy moustache. Look at my shiny, curved fangs. Grrrrrr! Don't I look ferocious? When a human comes near me, I rear back and lift my head and my front legs like this—in a striking position. See how fierce I look? When humans see me like this, they run away screaming."

"You'd be a real terror," the scorpion sneered, "if you were only as dangerous as you look."

"What do you mean! I *am* dangerous. I can kill frogs, toads, mice, and lizards, and I'm not even fully grown yet. I'm only six years old, and I won't reach my full growth for four more years. And you should see me jump. I can jump a jump almost two feet long."

30

"So you can jump. Big deal," the scorpion mocked. "Who cares about jumping? Jumping is for frogs."

The tarantula grew angrier and angrier. He waved his long front legs threateningly at the scorpion. "What are you doing here anyway, you pathetic little excuse for a lobster? This is *my* territory. You belong out on the desert."

"I didn't ask to be brought here," the scorpion snarled. "A stupid camper rolled me up in his sleeping bag and brought me into town. When he unrolled his sleeping bag, I gave him a sting he'll remember for a long, long time. With my beautiful poisonous tail." He looked admiringly at his tail, which was curled all the way over his head.

"I bite people, too, you know," the tarantula said, "or at least I could if I wanted to."

The scorpion waved his broad claws in derision. "I know you hairy spiders can bite people if you want to, and I'll admit your bite is painful, but it isn't fatal. On the other hand, scorpions have been known to *kill* human beings."

"Have you ever killed a human?" the tarantula ask.

"Well . . . no . . . but I *might* someday. This poison sting at the end of my tail is a powerful weapon." He curled it over his back in the stinging position. "Just look at that. Isn't it beautifully treacherous?"

"Talk, talk, talk! I don't think you're any more dangerous than I am," the tarantula declared.

"Ha! That's what *you* think. You should see me in action. Just wait until the next warm-blooded creature wanders past here. I'll show you how dangerous I am."

"I think something is coming right now," the tarantula whispered. "The grass is rustling."

Both of the fearsome creatures stood motionless, prepared to strike. Gustavus cautiously raised his head to see what was approaching through the tall grass. When the grass parted, he gasped in horror. He saw a soft, furry little animal which looked exactly like Mrs. Vole, and he knew immediately that it must be Mr. Vole returning from the day's food gathering. The little animal's cheeks were puffed out, filled with seeds. As Mr. Vole came closer, the scorpion raised his tail and prepared to strike.

Abandoning any attempt at caution, Gustavus leaped from his hiding place and screamed, "Turn around, Mr. Vole! You're in danger! Run away as fast as you can. *Run!"*

At the very first sound of Gustavus' voice, Mr. Vole changed his course, never missing a step. He raced back in the direction from which he'd come until he was no longer visible in the tall grass.

The tarantula and scorpion were startled and furious. They knew that neither of them was fast enough to catch the scampering vole. Stiff-legged, they danced a dance of rage, looking around in all directions to discover the culprit who had warned away their prey. But Gustavus had ducked back into the tunnel as soon as he saw that Mr. Vole was safe.

"Who shouted that warning?" the scorpion demanded.

"I have no idea," the tarantula answered. "But it sounded like a human voice. If there's a human around, we'd better leave this place. I don't want to get stepped on by a big human shoe."

"See! That's just what I was talking about," the scorpion scolded. "You may look ferocious, but the minute any danger comes near, you want to run away. Now

I'm afraid of nothing. If some human tried to stomp on me with his heavy shoe, I'd sting his ankle with my beautiful tail. . . ."

But Gustavus noticed that the scorpion was moving away, too, following the meeker tarantula toward the hot, graveled driveway.

Gustavus stayed in the tunnel for many minutes after the scorpion and the tarantula had vanished from sight. Then he crawled cautiously from his hiding place and headed once again in the direction of the cottonwood tree, this time looking ahead for any dangers in his path. The grass was tall enough to protect him from the scorching rays of the sun, but still so thick that Gustavus could hardly see where he was going. He had pushed his way between the high green blades for nearly a quarter of an hour when he suddenly broke through to a clearing.

"This must be the flower bed," he realized. "It will be a relief to get out of that tall grass and onto some good old dirt." The flowers, which had looked delicate and colorful when he was five feet tall, now loomed high above his head like bright, enormous jungle trees. He made his way to an azalea shrub and sat down to rest at its base.

"Hallelujah, brother!"

Gustavus jumped up and looked around him.

"Peace be with you. *Shalom.*"

He raised his head and stared directly into a green, triangular face with enormous bulging eyes. Between the bulging eyes, just behind the base of two long, wandlike antennae, were three smaller eyes arranged in a triangle.

"Allah be praised. *Hare Krishna.*"

The voice was coming from a mouth at the bottom of the triangular head. Gustavus stretched back his neck to see the rest of the strange creature's body. It was long like a thin, green stick and the same color as the azalea leaves. The creature was clinging head-down on the stem of the shrub.

"Who are you?" Gustavus asked.

"Glory be! I am Brother Mantis. Let me come down from this perch so that we can become better acquainted."

The insect moved daintily on long, skinny legs which looked like stilts joined at angles. He came to a halt on the ground beside Gustavus, holding his thick, spiked forelegs bent under his chin as though he were praying.

"And who might you be, little brother?" the insect asked Gustavus.

"I'm Gustavus Bell."

"The heavens be praised, Brother Gustavus. Welcome to the fold. Brighten the corner where you are."

"I beg your pardon?" Gustavus stammered.

"It is just my way of speaking, Brother Gustavus. I belong to the largest religious order in the world, *Mantis religiosa,* the brotherhood of praying mantises. We make a habit of wearing green, although some of the brothers wear brown. We pray all the time, in order to finish all the prayers which human beings have dropped."

"You say *human* prayers, Brother Mantis?" Gustavus asked.

"Oh my, my yes! Saying human prayers is the life's work of all praying mantises."

"But why?"

"You see, little brother, prayers which are only half-finished do NOT wing their way to heaven. Oh my my no, not at all. Half-finished prayers merely drop to the earth, like so many beads from a broken necklace. It is the never-ending duty of my brother mantises and myself to pick up the broken prayers and string them back together, so to speak. And there are so many unfinished prayers. . . ." Brother Mantis sighed and shook his head on his long green neck. "Each year, each month, each day and night, more and more prayers drop unfinished on the ground. Little children fall asleep in the middle of their prayers. Grown-ups become distracted halfway through a line. I fear that someday, brother, there will be more broken prayers than there are mantises to put them back together again. Lord have mercy!"

"May I listen to you pray, Brother Mantis?" Gustavus asked.

"Glory, glory, hallelujah. Of course you may, little brother." The praying mantis extended his forelegs in a reverent manner and swayed from side to side. "By the hair of Siva, give us this day. *Krishna Krishna.* We are gathered together. If I die before I wake, the mountain will come to Muhammad. *Hospodi pomiluy.* Let us offer each other the sign of peace. God bless Mommy, Daddy, and Great Aunt Kate. Confucius say, 'Treat inferiors with dignity.' Let us bow to the east. Hear, O Israel, yang and yin. Praise the Lord. Hallelujah!"

"But Brother Mantis," Gustavus interrupted, "your prayers are all mixed up! They're all in a jumble."

"That's the way we get them, little brother," the praying mantis replied. "Broken prayers always fall to the earth in a jumble. If we mantises took the time to sort them out, we'd never get them all reprayed. So we

37

just put them all together any which way and send them off to heaven. We must be doing things right, little brother. We've never had any complaints from heaven."

Gustavus sat and thought about this while the mantis went on mumbling his prayers. The prayers were oddly soothing to his ears, and he relaxed and listened for a long while. When at last he stood up he felt refreshed, ready to continue his journey to the cottonwood tree.

"Brother Mantis," he said, "I have a long, hard journey ahead through the wilderness. Will you offer some of your prayers for me?"

"Glory be, brother!" the praying mantis shouted. "You can bet I will. Of course of course of course. I'll pray you to safety, little brother. Yea, verily. Count on me."

"Thank you, Brother Mantis. I'll be leaving now."

"Love and peace, brother," the mantis called after Gustavus. *"Dominus vobiscum. Shalom."*

As Gustavus turned to wave, he heard the mantis intoning, "Yea, though I walk through the valley of the shadow of . . ."

The distance to the cottonwood tree looked unbearably long. "But I've got to get back there," Gustavus told himself. "If I don't get back under the tree, Fearless and my mother won't know where to look for me. And if they start looking all over the yard, they might step on me and they'd never know it. Ugh! Squashed like a bug!"

The thought was enough to make him hurry faster.

38

His body became soaked with perspiration, and he felt terribly thirsty. The heat of the sun burned deep into his flesh, and soon his head began to spin and he went into another shrinking spell.

"Oh no! Not again," he sobbed. "I'll never make it back to the tree." He fell onto the ground and let the dizziness sweep through his body. After it had passed, he remained on the ground. "I've got to figure out how tall I am now," he thought. "Let me see. I was seven and a half inches tall when Fearless left me under the tree. Then I had a shrinking spell after I drank the water in the voles' house, so I would have been three and three quarters inches tall. I had another spell when those terrible worms touched me in the tunnel, which would have made me one and seven eighths inches. And I just had another, so that means I'm fifteen sixteenths of an inch tall. To make it easier, I'll just say that I'm one inch tall now."

He lay still for a moment, fighting the fear which rose in him, fear that he'd never see his parents or his home again. Then he made a strong effort to calm himself. "There must be some way to get back," he thought, "but I'll never think of it lying here feeling sorry for myself."

He rose slowly to his feet. The stems of grass towered far above his head. He pulled four blades of grass together, enough, he calculated, to hold his slight weight, and climbed to the top of them to see what he could see. The nearest landmark was a dandelion growing a foot away from him.

"If I can get to that dandelion, I can climb to the top of it and get my bearings. It's more than twice as tall as this grass."

Gustavus walked toward the dandelion. The blades

of grass seemed much more widely spaced now that he was so small, but the distances between objects were much greater. At last he reached the stem of the dandelion. After resting for a few minutes to catch his breath, he began to climb. The stem of the dandelion was smooth and hard to hold, but Gustavus climbed carefully, hand over hand, until he reached the top. He was careful to stay in the shade underneath the bright yellow blossom so that the hot sunlight wouldn't reach him and bring on another spell. From his vantage point eight inches above ground he could see the cottonwood tree, but it looked a vast distance away.

"Hey there, boy."

The voice startled Gustavus so much that he lost his handhold, slid down the stem of the dandelion, and landed in the dirt. A fly with a shiny, metallic-looking body floated down lazily and landed beside him.

"Don't be scared, boy. I saw you climbin' that dandelion and I thought I'd just drift over and say howdy, friendly-like. By dingies, you are a *little* feller. What's your name, boy?"

"Gustavus Bell."

"Well, I'll just call you Gus. Let me introduce myself, Gus. I'm a blue bottle fly, but my friends call me Blue. I'd be pleased if you'd do the same."

"Glad to know you, Blue."

"Glad to know *you*, Gus." The fly extended his right front leg, and they shook hands. "How'd you get so goldang *little*, Gus?"

"Oh, I've got some kind of crazy sickness called halving disease. I keep getting these dizzy spells, and then I shrink in half. I used to be five feet tall, and now look at me."

"Well, shucks," Blue drawled, "you can't be more than an inch!"

"A little less, to be exact," Gustavus corrected him.

"My, my. I ain't never seen nothin' like this before. You live around here, Gus?"

"I live in that red brick house over there, or at least I used to, before this awful thing happened to me."

"That there's a right pretty house," Blue commented. "I been inside it a couple of times. But me, I prefer the outdoors, so I mostly live out here in the yard. I didn't always live here, though. I was born on a ranch about twenty, thirty miles outside of town."

"I think I would have guessed that," Gustavus said.

"We was always ranch folk," Blue went on. "Why, my daddy's family has lived on the same spread for a hundred or more generations. Most of my brothers is still out there on the ranch. But me, I had a hankerin' for city life, so one day I hitched a ride on a horse trailer and come into town. Didn't like it once I got there, though. Too much noise, and exhaust fumes from cars makin' it hard to breathe. So I flew out here to the suburbs, and I like it pretty good here. Course, it was a mite hard gettin' used to the change in diet. On the ranch I ate locusts, mostly, but nowadays I live on popsicle sticks and lollipops that kids has dropped, with maybe an occasional banana peel or apple core."

"Do you ever think you'd like to go back to the ranch?" Gustavus asked.

"No, Gus, I don't think so," Blue replied, rubbing

his front legs together. "I'm content to live out my days in this here backyard."

Gustavus sighed. "I'm beginning to think I'll have to live out my days in this backyard, too."

"Where would you rather be?" Blue asked.

"At first I wanted to go over to that cottonwood tree, but now that I've grown so small, I think I'd rather go back into my house. But it's so far away that I'll never reach it."

"Well, don't fret, boy," the fly said. "I can take you there. There's most always a window screen that don't fit properly that I can get through. You can climb up on my back and I'll take you where you want."

"But won't I be too heavy for you?"

"Maybe right now you'd be too heavy, but from what you've been tellin' me, you're likely to shrink again, and if you was just half the size you are right now, I wouldn't have no trouble carryin' you."

"That's really kind of you, Blue."

"Think nothin' of it. Us Westerners always try to help a creature in trouble, even a wee bitty little human feller."

Gustavus thought hard for a moment. "Maybe I could hurry up the shrinking process. It seems that every time I get into the hot sun, I have a shrinking spell. If I climb this dandelion again, and get on top of the flower in the bright sunlight, I'll probably shrink in half, and then I'll be the right size for you."

"You do what you think best, boy."

Gustavus climbed the dandelion stem a second time, but this time when he got to the top, he reached around the large outer petals and grasped the soft, fleshy petals in the center of the blossom. He pulled himself onto the

42

top and lay flat on his back, his feet sticking over the edge, his face turned up to the sun. He felt a little nervous. It was the first time he had deliberately tried to bring on a shrinking spell, and he hated to do it. But he desperately wanted to get home, and this seemed the only possible way.

The heat of the sun sank into his body. In less than a minute he began to grow dizzy. When he noticed that his feet were no longer over the edge of the blossom, but that his whole body was centered in the soft yellow petals, he knew that he had shrunk to half an inch.

"I'm ready, Blue."

"Okay, Gus," the fly called out. "Don't bother coming down. I'll come up there and get you." The fly flew up and landed gently on the head of the dandelion, next to Gustavus.

"Now, boy, before we start out, I want to give you some instructions. File our flight plan, so to speak. I'm the pilot and you're the passenger. You'll have to sit on my back right behind my head, up in front of the wings. You can hang onto them spiny hairs growin' out of my back. But whatever you do, don't touch my halteres."

"Your what?"

"My halteres. They're like a second pair of wings, only real, real tiny. They're just behind my wings. They're my stabilizin' system, and they work just like gyroscopes. They keep me balanced when I'm flyin'. They have to vibrate all the time I'm airborne. If you grab onto them, I'll lose my balance, and we'll crash."

"I'll be careful, Blue. I promise."

"Okay, pardner. Climb aboard."

Gustavus climbed onto the fly's back and seated himself just ahead of the thin, lightly veined wings. The spiny

43

hairs on Blue's back were uncomfortable to sit on, but they made good handholds.

"All set, Gus?" Blue called.

"All set, Blue. Ready for takeoff."

Blue lifted off smoothly from the dandelion blossom and began to circle. The buzzing of the fly in flight was much louder than Gustavus had expected, and it began to make his ears ring.

"Hey, Blue!" he shouted above the roar. "Can you quiet down the engine a little bit?"

"Can't make it any quieter, Gus," Blue shouted back. "That's the way the durn thing operates."

"Hey, Blue," Gustavus yelled again. "Do you have to keep flying around in circles? It's making me dizzy."

"Us flies always fly in circles," Blue hollered. "It's just the way we do things. But I'll get you to where you're goin', boy. Don't you fret. Just remember, *keep your hands off them halteres!*"

Blue soared higher and higher. Gustavus tried to catch sight of his house, to see how far away it was, but the world was whirling around in a blur.

"Blue!" he screamed. "I'm going to have another spell!"

"Try to hang on, boy," the fly roared. "We're nearly there."

But Gustavus couldn't hang on. He felt himself shrinking, and he began to slide backwards. He tried to find something to hold onto, and he did—a transparent, shell-shaped projection behind Blue's wing.

"Let go, boy! Let go!" Blue bellowed. "You've got ahold of one of my halteres. Let 'er go or I'll go into a spin. Hot dingies! I'm a-goin' to crash! Let go, boy, before it's too late!"

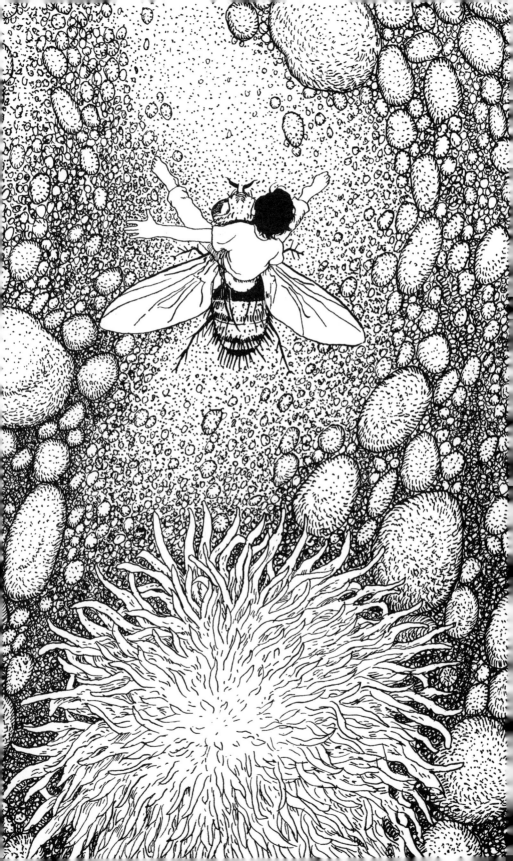

Gustavus let go. As he fell through the air, he spun around and around. He had just enough time to think, "This is the end," when he landed with a splash in a pool of water. He stood up, spluttering, trying to shake the water from his ears and his eyes.

"Hi, Bud," a voice said from somewhere near.

"I'm not Bud. My name is Gustavus," he said, trying to see who had spoken to him.

"When I saw you on this rosebush, I thought you were a bud," the voice said. *"Ha ha ha!* What's the matter, pal? You're not laughing."

"You wouldn't laugh, either, if you'd fallen out of the sky and landed in a puddle. Is that where I am, on a rosebush? Then why did I land in a puddle?"

"It wasn't a puddle, pal. It was just a drop of water left over from this morning's watering. It's a good thing you landed in it. It broke your fall."

"Where are you, anyway?" Gustavus asked, twisting and turning to see where the voice was coming from.

"I'm up here, on the stem. I'm the same color as the stem. That's why you can't see me. Look hard, up this way."

Gustavus strained his eyes, and there, on the stem just above his head, he saw a bright green aphid.

"Oh, I see you now. Hey, that's pretty clever camouflage."

"It's not camouflage, pal. It's called protective coloration."

"Oh, excuse me. Say, could you do me a favor? I

46

have this condition known as halving disease. I keep shrinking in half. The last time I knew for sure, I was a half inch tall. Then I had another shrinking spell, which would have made me a quarter of an inch. But when I was falling through the air, I was spinning around so much that I couldn't tell whether I had another spell or not. So I wonder if you could tell me whether I look a quarter of an inch tall or an eighth of an inch tall right now."

"What do you think I am," the aphid asked, "an inchworm? *Ha ha ha ha!* You're not laughing again, pal. That was a joke. When I tell a joke, *everyone* laughs."

"Oh sorry," Gustavus apologized. "Ha ha ha. That was really pretty funny."

"Well, pal," the aphid said, looking Gustavus up and down with his tiny, jet-black eyes, "I'd judge you're pretty close to an eighth of an inch tall."

"Oh boy," Gustavus groaned, "this is hopeless. I might as well just give up."

"You got troubles, pal?" the aphid asked. "Tell me about them. Maybe I can help."

Gustavus, incredulous, stared at the tiny green bug. *"You!* Help *me!"*

The aphid waved his antennae lazily. "You'd be surprised, pal. I got connections you wouldn't dream of. But let's get down to business. What did you say your name is?"

"Gustavus."

"Glad to know you, Gus Davis. My name is Alphonso Aphid, but everyone calls me Big Al."

"Big Al? *Big?"* Gustavus' voice rose in disbelief.

"Look, Gus Davis, I realize that even though you're only an eighth of an inch tall, you're still twice as big as

I am. But size is relative. In the aphid world I'm a big man, and I don't mean size-wise. I'm the boss of the A.A.A.A.—the Association of Allied American Aphids. I control all the aphid and plant lice activity that takes place either on or underneath this rosebush. So if you treat me right—well, maybe we can do business."

"I don't understand, Big Al."

"Let me explain, Gus Davis. You got a problem, so you come to me for help. Okay. I pull a few strings, and I get you the help you need. I do you a favor, then you do me a favor."

"But Big Al, how can you possibly help me?"

"Let me worry about that, pal. You just tell me what your problem is."

"Well, my problem is that I want to go home, and I don't know how I'll ever get there."

"Where do you live, Gus Davis?"

"I live in that red brick house over there, with my father and my mother and my dog Fearless."

"Is your father that tall, bald-headed guy with the horn-rimmed glasses?"

"Yes, that's my dad."

"Hmmmmmmmm. Let me think about this for a minute." Big Al's antennae waved more rapidly. "Uh huh! I got it. Now as I explained to you, we make a deal. I promise to get you back to your house, and you do me a favor in return."

"Anything, Big Al. I'd do anything for you if you could get me back into my own bedroom."

"Then here's the deal. You make your old man promise to quit spraying this rosebush with insect killer. Every time he comes out here with that can of bug juice, I lose a thousand of my boys."

"What about the other rosebushes?" Gustavus asked. "Do you want my dad to quit spraying them, too?"

"That's out of my territory. The aphids on those other bushes belong to different families," Big Al replied. "Let them make their own arrangements. I only worry about my own guys."

"Okay, Big Al. It's a deal. But I still can't see how you're going to get me home."

"I told you, Gus Davis. I got connections all over. In the entertainment field, for instance, I practically run the glowworm union."

"Funny," Gustavus said, "I never thought of glowworms as entertainers."

"Are you kidding?" Big Al roared. "They're the biggest hams in show business. Get 'em in front of an audience and you can't turn 'em off. *Ha ha ha ha!*"

Gustavus giggled.

"Now where was I? Oh yeah, about my connections. In the transportation industry—by the way, pal, what do you want? Air or ground transportation?"

"Well," Gustavus considered, scratching his head, "flying's faster, but the last time I flew I fell off and landed here. So maybe ground transportation would be safer."

"Done!" Big Al declared. "I'll have my boys get in touch with the ants—that's our ground transportation department. They mostly just carry freight, but we can persuade them to take a passenger this one time. If they don't, their plant lice will go on strike."

"Their plant lice?"

Big Al sighed impatiently. "Gus Davis, you don't know much about the insect world, do you?"

Gustavus shook his head, embarrassed.

49

"Then listen and maybe you'll learn something. Every variety of aphids and plant lice secretes a sweet, sticky stuff called honeydew. All the ants go crazy over honeydew. The ants even keep their own herds of plant lice, and milk them for honeydew like a farmer milks a cow, only the ants do the milking by stroking the plant lice with their antennae. They even build little pens out of mud to keep their herds in."

Gustavus nodded. "But what does all this have to do with me?"

"Simple. We tell the ants we want them to carry you back to your house. If the ants object, we send out an order to the plant lice to stop the production of honeydew. The ants don't want their supply of honeydew cut off, so they do what we ask them. Understand?"

Gustavus nodded in amazement.

"I'll start making the arrangements right now," Big Al said. "By the way, pal, which room do you want to be delivered to?"

"My bedroom is the one with the blue carpet."

"I'll let the ants work out the details. Ants are smart little guys," Big Al assured him. "They might even know a cure for your halving disease."

Big Al was facing upward on the stem of the rose-bush. "Hey Louie!" he called.

"Yeah, boss?" The voice came down from above.

"Send out word to the ants that we want to meet with them about a transportation problem."

"Right, boss."

Big Al turned to Gustavus. "One thing about this aphid operation, we got a very good communications system. Our boys are strung out all the way up and down the stem of this rosebush."

50

"Very efficient," Gustavus remarked.

Big Al said, "It will take me a few minutes to get things arranged. Would you like to look around a bit? There's an old dame who lives on the end of this cluster of leaves. She's always complaining that no one ever visits her. Why don't you go and keep her company while I make contact with the ants?"

"Okay," Gustavus answered. "How do I get there?"

"Just keep going until you reach the last leaf. You'll find her. She's always at home."

Gustavus got down on his hands and knees and crawled along the prickly center stem of the leaf cluster. Just before he got to the final leaf he heard a high, trembling voice calling, "This way, this way, young man. Have you come to visit me? Do come in. I love visitors."

He looked up and saw an orange and black spotted ladybug sitting in the center of the leaf.

"Come along, come along," she urged him. "Sit right here beside me and we can have a nice chat." She sighed. "It's so seldom that a nice young man comes to pass the time of day."

"How do you do, Ma'am," Gustavus said.

"You must address me by my title," she told him. "I'm royalty, you know. Lady Bug. You must address me as Lady Bug."

"Pleased to meet you, Lady Bug."

"You have lovely manners, young man. Most children today have terrible manners. You wouldn't believe the abuse I must put up with." She sniffed delicately.

"Abuse, Ma'am?"

51

"Don't call me Ma'am. Call me My Lady. I'm royalty, you know."

"Yes, My Lady, you told me that. But you said that you must put up with abuse. What do you mean?" he asked.

"Well!" She sniffed again, louder. "All summer long children take me in their little hands. I don't mind that at all, you understand. I enjoy the company of young folks. When they pick me up, I always hope that we'll have a nice visit—a nice little chat. But then the nasty children always say the same thing. They say, 'Ladybug, Ladybug, fly away home. Your house is on fire and your children will burn.' Can you imagine! Such a terrible thing to say! Well brought up boys and girls would never say such a thing."

"But they don't mean to offend you, My Lady," Gustavus protested.

"Don't mean to *offend* me! When they tell me to go away and then say that my poor children are going to be burned up! How would your mother like it, young man, if every time she went out on the street little children told her to go home because her house was in flames and that *you* were going to be burned to a cinder?"

"But My Lady, it's just a harmless little nursery rhyme."

"A lot you know!" Lady Bug gave a tiny sob. "You may think it's only a harmless little nursery rhyme, but it's true history, young man, true history! In England many of the ladybugs lived on hop vines. The hop vines were our ancestral homes. And every autumn, at harvest time, the hop vines were set on fire. Of course all of the ladybugs had to fly away from the burning vines, but our poor little children, who were too young to fly, had to

53

crawl to safety as best they could. Many of them actually were burned to death. That's how that dreadful verse got started. And you say it's just a harmless little nursery rhyme!"

"I'm sorry, My Lady," Gustavus apologized. "I didn't know that."

"I accept your apology, young man. But oh, it's such a lonely life, always being rejected and told to fly away." She began to weep loudly, and Gustavus began to feel very uncomfortable.

"Well, I'd better be going now," he said. "Big Al is waiting for me."

"You see!" she wailed. "You can't spare even a few minutes to visit with a poor old lady."

Gustavus took a deep breath. "My Lady, I don't want to sound disrespectful to my elders. But maybe if you were a little more cheerful, you'd have more company."

Lady Bug stared at him with her round black eyes. "Do you really think so, young man?"

"Of course. If you're always sad, and always talking about your troubles, people will naturally stay away from you. My mother always says, 'Laugh and the world laughs with you. Cry and you cry alone.'"

"I never thought of it that way. Perhaps you're right." She raised her orange and black wings. "I'll give it a try. I'll fly across this bush and visit some of my acquaintances. And I'll practice laughing on the way. Tee hee. Tee hee hee. Good by, young man. Thank you for the advice. Tee hee hee."

"Good by, My Lady. Good luck!" Gustavus waved as Lady Bug flew from the leaf. Then he turned and crawled back to Big Al.

"Back again, Gus Davis?" Big Al asked. "Did you have a nice visit with Lady Bug? She's a nice old dame, but a bit weepy. I'm still working on the arrangements with the ants. Why don't you just relax? Would you like some honeydew?"

"No thanks," Gustavus replied. "I'll just drink some of this water I fell into when I first arrived. This halving disease makes me terribly thirsty."

He leaned over the drop of water to drink. Just at that precise moment the sun, in its slow march across the August sky, cast a ray of light over the edge of an overhanging leaf which had been shading Gustavus. The ray of sunlight reflected brilliantly in the drop of water, which shone so dazzlingly in Gustavus' eyes that he became violently dizzy, shrank in half, and fell into the water. The combined shock of the sun's heat, the brilliant glare, and the fall into the water brought on a whole series of shrinking spells. Gustavus' head was spinning, and then his whole body seemed to be tumbling, at first in wide circles, and then in circles which grew narrower and narrower. Above the roar of the water, Gustavus could hear Big Al's voice shouting faintly, "Don't worry, Gus Davis. We'll get you back home. I gave you my promise, and Big Al always keeps his promises."

Gustavus was no longer having spells of shrinking in half. His shrinking was now a continuous state, and he panicked. Fear gripped him so thoroughly that he could no longer think. He held himself rigid, clenching his fists so hard that his fingernails dug trenches in his

55

palms. After a long while the sounds around him seemed to subside. He forced himself to relax and to surrender to the forces of nature which were controlling him so completely against his will. He seemed to be borne on some sort of tide. The first thought that came to him was that he no longer felt wet. He opened his eyes, which had been tightly shut. All around him were balls, millions of balls slithering and sliding over him and over each other.

He could distinguish that the balls were in groups— big balls, which looked to him about the size of tenpin bowling balls, and on each big one two smaller balls about the size of baseballs. The baseballs were attached to the bowling balls, two of the smaller balls jutting out like rabbit ears from each of the larger ones. The groups of balls were tightly packed around him and were in a constant state of motion.

Gustavus was extremely puzzled, but then his brain suddenly grasped the amazing truth. He was so small that he was seeing actual molecules of water. The big balls were oxygen atoms, and the smaller balls were atoms of hydrogen. Even as he realized what he was viewing, he continued to shrink, and the balls grew larger and larger.

"Is this ever going to end?" he asked himself. He tried to grab one of the atoms to steady himself, but he was unable to hold on as the atom grew more and more tremendous. He had no idea how much time had elapsed since he fell into the drop of water, but it seemed like hours. He began to see spheres within spheres. He felt weightless. He was floating head over heels in space around a core of something he couldn't comprehend, while a tiny speck of energy whirled around him at a great distance away from him.

He tried to force his memory to recall what he had

learned about the structure of atoms in his seventh grade science class. "That core must be the nucleus of an atom," he thought, "and the particle of energy whirling around it must be an electron. Since there's only one electron whirling around, I must be inside an atom of hydrogen. I'll bet I'm the first human being who's ever been inside an atom. But I probably won't get back to tell about it."

He continued to be tossed inside the electronic pull of the hydrogen atom, and he found himself almost enjoying the strange sights and sensations. Then a horrible thought occurred to him. "I'm still shrinking. I can feel it. But an atom is the smallest thing known to man! If I get smaller than an atom, I'll just shrink into oblivion . . . and here . . . I . . . *go!*"

"Gustavus."

"Gustavus!"

At first he didn't believe it, but he was actually hearing voices. They sounded like the voices of his mother and his father calling his name. He was lying flat on his back. There was something solid beneath him. He pressed his hands hard against whatever was supporting him. It felt like his cotton bedspread. He stretched his hands above his head. His fingers touched his maple headboard. He stretched his feet, and his toes touched his maple footboard.

"He's coming out of it," his father's voice said.

"Gustavus, wake up!"

He opened his eyes and saw his mother hovering over him. Her expression was one of deep concern.

"Hi," he said weakly.

"Oh Gustavus, we've been so worried," his mother said.

"What happened?" he asked.

"That's what we've been wondering. I had to stay much longer than I expected at the church," she explained. "Only three women showed up to do all the decorating, and we didn't finish until seven o'clock. When I came up the stairs from the church basement, I found Fearless waiting at the door. He looked hot and thirsty and miserable, as though he'd been waiting for me for hours. I thought something might be wrong, so I hurried home. When I came inside and saw that you hadn't turned on the oven, I knew something must have happened to you."

"The oven!" Gustavus exclaimed. "I forgot all about the oven."

"It doesn't matter, Son," his father assured him.

"I hurried into your bedroom, and I found you lying on your bed," his mother continued. "And it was so strange. There were ants all over your room, dozens of them, crawling every which way on your blue carpet. One of them was even beside you on your bed. And—I know this sounds silly—but the ant on your bed looked wet. In fact, there was a tiny damp spot on the bedspread where the ant was standing."

Gustavus smiled faintly.

"I ran to the kitchen to get the can of ant spray, leaving you alone in the room with Fearless, and when I came back all the ants were gone! And Fearless was gone too."

Gustavus dropped his hand over the edge of the bed and stroked Fearless' cold nose. "He must have carried the ants to safety," he thought. "Good old Fearless!" The dog licked his hand.

"Just about that time I came home," his father broke in. "Mother and I both tried to wake you, but you wouldn't wake up. You felt feverish, so Mother called Dr. Turner."

"The doctor said you must have had a touch of sunstroke. Were you out riding your bike this afternoon without anything covering your head?"

"Yes, Mom," Gustavus admitted.

"I've told you time and time again to keep your head covered in the hot sunlight. No wonder you got sunstroke! The temperature was a hundred and ten degrees this afternoon—in the shade!"

"I'm sorry," he whispered.

"Dr. Turner said you're to rest in bed, take two aspirin tablets every four hours, and drink plenty of fluids."

"There's a fly in this room," his father announced.

Gustavus jumped up in bed. "What kind of fly? Is it a blue bottle fly?"

"I don't know," his father answered. "I can't tell one fly from another." He moved toward the door. "I'll get a newspaper and swat it."

"No, Dad!" Gustavus yelled. "Please don't swat that fly! Open the window screen a little bit so he can fly outside."

His father looked bewildered. "But why, Gustavus?"

Gustavus clutched his middle. "Dad, I'm so sick that the sight of blood, even fly blood, would make me throw up. Ugh!"

Shaking his head, his father walked to the window and opened the screen. Gustavus relaxed on the bed and closed his eyes, listening as the sound of the fly's buzzing grew fainter and fainter until it vanished outside. He opened his eyes again. "Dad, will you promise me something?"

"What, Son?"

"You know that rosebush just next to the back porch, the one with roses that are half pink and half yellow? Please promise me that you'll never spray that bush again with insecticide."

"Why not?"

"It's . . . it's a vow I made. For . . . ecology!"

"What about the other rosebushes?" his father asked. "Do you want me to stop spraying them, too?"

"Let them make their own arrangements," Gustavus replied.

His father gave his mother a look which meant, "The boy still isn't right in the head."

His mother gave his father a look which meant, "Perhaps we'd better humor him."

"All right, Gustavus. I won't spray that one rosebush ever again," his father promised.

"Shake hands on it?" Gustavus pleaded.

"Shake!" His father shook Gustavus' hand to seal the promise.

"Please lie down and rest, honey," his mother coaxed, gently pushing his head against the pillow. "We've done what you asked. We let the fly out, and Daddy promised that he won't spray the rosebush. Everything has been taken care of."

Gustavus burrowed his head into the pillow and sighed contentedly. Mr. Vole was safe, the ants were safe,

Blue was safe, and his father had promised that he wouldn't spray Big Al's rosebush. And best of all, Gustavus was five feet tall once again.

"You're right, Mom," he said. "I can rest now. Everything has been taken care of."